# I Wonder
# If Dragons Are Real

• • • • • • • • • • • • • • • • • • • •
**and other neat facts about** reptiles & amphibians

By Annabelle Donati
Illustrated by Suzanne Barnes

A GOLDEN BOOK • NEW YORK
Western Publishing Company, Inc., Racine, Wisconsin 53404

Produced by Graymont Enterprises, Inc., Norfolk, Connecticut
Producer: *Ruth Lerner Perle*
Design: *Michele Italiano-Perla*
Cover Illustration: *Jean Cassels*
Editorial consultant: *John Behler,* Curator of Herpetology, New York Zoological Society, New York

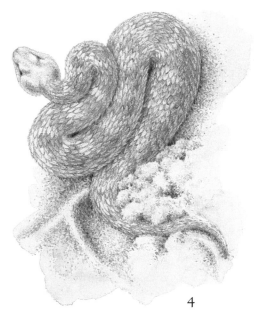

# Contents

# What does it take to be a reptile?

Snakes slither, lizards break off their tails, turtles crawl, crocodiles have huge snapping jaws, and chameleons can change color. Each of these animals can do something the others can't, but they are all reptiles and in some ways they are alike.

alligator

chameleon

## Reptiles have:

### Dry scales or plates
A reptile's body is covered with dry scales or bony plates that often overlap like shingles. Some have both scales and plates.

### Short legs or none at all
Most reptiles crawl close to the ground, though some can run upright on their hind legs. Snakes have no legs at all.

### Skin that sheds
A reptile's old skin comes off from time to time and a new one grows in its place. This is called *shedding*.

### Leathery eggs
Most reptiles lay eggs that have tough, leathery shells. Some give birth to live babies.

### "Cold" blood
A reptile's body temperature changes with the temperature of its surroundings. That means its blood can get very cold or very hot!

turtle

snake

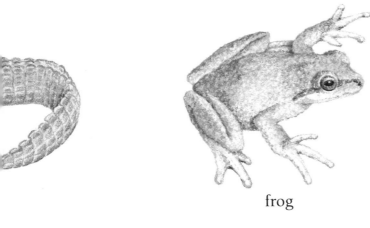
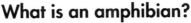

## What is an amphibian?

Amphibians are a group of animals that usually begin their life in water and then live on land as adults. Most are born with gills, like fish, and then develop lungs for life out of water. Frogs, toads, newts, and salamanders are amphibians. Unlike reptiles, most amphibians have soft, smooth skin.

frog

salamander

## Is a worm a reptile?

No. Since worms have no legs, they are sometimes confused with snakes.
But worms are not reptiles.
Like reptiles, worms are cold-blooded. But unlike reptiles, they do not have scales or skeletons.

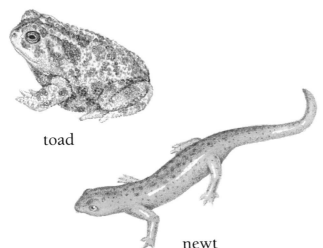

toad

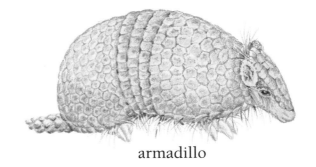

newt

armadillo

## Is an armadillo a reptile?

No. An armadillo's body is covered with horny plates that look like a reptile's scales. But armadillos are mammals. They are warm-blooded and nurse their young with mother's milk.

## Tell Me More

The largest and strangest-looking reptiles ever to walk the earth were dinosaurs, which lived millions of years ago. Dinosaurs are *extinct*—meaning there are none living today.

Styracosaurus

# How do snakes travel?

Since snakes don't have legs, they can't walk, but they do manage to crawl by moving their large belly plates. These plates are attached to their ribs by muscles that push the snakes along. Snakes have several ways of moving their long, muscular bodies:

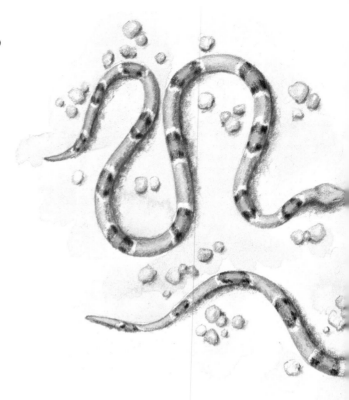

A thick snake has broad, flat scales on the underside of its belly. These scales can grip the ground and push the snake forward.

A snake can wriggle forward by pushing itself against rocks and trees.

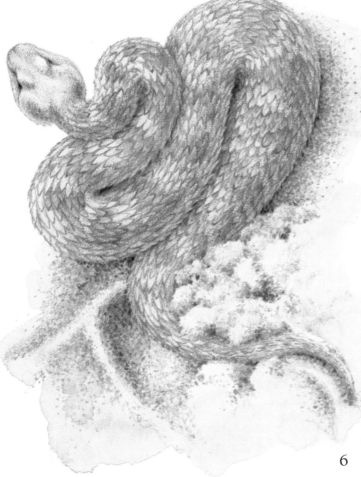

## Amazing *but* TRUE

Scientists believe that snakes had legs millions of years ago, when dinosaurs lived. Pythons still have little spurs at the rear of the body where their legs used to be.

6

A snake can bunch itself in tight, accordionlike loops and thrust its head forward, pulling the rest of its body along.

## Tell Me More

The sidewinder rattlesnake lives in the sandy desert. Since it is hard for the sidewinder to get a grip on the loose sand, this snake has to move its body in a special way. First it throws its head forward and anchors it in the sand. Then it flips its body forward and lands farther ahead. It moves sideways and leaves J-shaped marks in the sand.

## Snakes are special in many ways:

**No ears**
Snakes can't hear sounds through the air, but they can feel vibrations if something is coming their way.

**No eyelids**
Snakes can't close their eyes or blink.

**Forked tongues**
A snake's moist tongue picks up scents and transfers them to smell organs in its mouth.

**Terrific teeth**
Snakes have sharp teeth for grasping, but they can't chew. They swallow their prey whole.

**Stretchy jaws**
A snake's jaws can unhinge. It can open its mouth wide enough to stretch around prey larger than itself.

**Tenderizer stomachs**
Snakes have strong juices in their body that can soften the bones and skin of prey they have swallowed.

**Double-jointed joints**
Snakes can coil their body in any direction.

**Stupendous skeletons**
Snakes have hundreds of ribs attached to long backbones.

**Special skin**
A snake grows a new skin several times a year.

**Magnificent markings**
Snake scales are arranged like roof shingles and come in a great variety of colors and patterns.

# Are all snakes dangerous?

Snakes are *carnivores* and must kill other animals for food. Like all animals, snakes have special weapons to help them do this. Some catch their prey with their jaws and and then gulp it down. Some use venom to stun or kill their prey. Others wrap their bodies around their victims and smother them.

Most snakes hunt small animals, such as frogs, lizards, and mice. Some even eat other snakes. But they attack human beings only to protect themselves. Most snakes are very useful to people, since they kill rats, mice, and other animals that destroy crops and carry disease.

## Which snakes have no poison?

There are hundreds of kinds of nonpoisonous snakes living in many different parts of the world.

The hognose snake lives in the eastern part of North America. It is a harmless snake, but it looks fierce. When it is threatened, the hognose hisses, flattens its neck, and pretends it is about to strike. This is usually enough to frighten its enemies away. But if this trick doesn't work, the snake rolls over and plays dead.

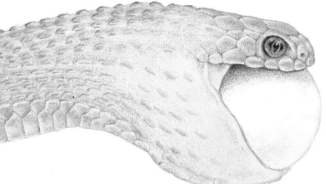

# Amazing but TRUE

The African egg-eating snake steals eggs from nests and swallows them whole. This snake has a row of sharp, pointy bones in its throat that punch holes in the eggshell. The snake then swallows the inside of the egg and spits out the shell.

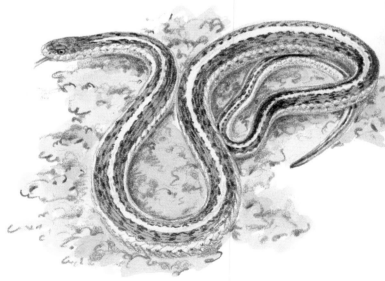

The garter snake lives near water and in grassy areas in North America. Nonpoisonous garter snakes and their relatives are more common and better known than any other snake.

8

The western yellowbelly racer is known for its beautiful colors. It lives in bushes and trees and feeds on birds, frogs, and other small creatures.

### How does a poisonous snake kill its prey?

A poisonous snake has special glands that make poison, or *venom*. These glands connect to long, hollow, pointed teeth called *fangs*. The fangs are shaped like tiny funnels. They have a wide opening at the top end and a small hole near the tip. The poison glands push venom into the wide top end of the fang. When the snake bites, the venom comes out through the tip of the fang and is injected into the prey.

The mud snake's tail is sharp at its tip, but it is not poisonous. This snake lives in swamps and feeds on fish and frogs.

# Does the king cobra wear a crown?

Although no cobra wears a crown, cobras do have hoods! Hoods are flaps of skin that can be spread out to look like headdresses. An angry king cobra is an awesome sight. It raises its body, spreads its hood, and hisses loudly at its attacker.

## Tell Me More

The female king cobra is the only snake that builds a nest to keep her eggs warm until they hatch.

When baby cobras hatch, they are already equipped with enough venom to start hunting and killing small snakes.

## Heads up!

The cobra can move forward with its head raised and the front of its body lifted off the ground.

## Charmed, I'm sure

Snake charmers can make cobras sway from side to side when they play a flute. But the snake can't hear a thing, since it is deaf. It watches the flute and moves as the flute moves.

## Amazing but TRUE

The spitting cobra can squirt venom into its victim's eyes to blind it.

# What is a boa constrictor?

Rattlesnakes, cobras, and other poisonous snakes kill their prey by injecting it with venom. The boa has no poison, but it has another weapon—strength. When it winds its body around its victim, the boa squeezes so hard that it smothers it. Then the boa swallows its prey whole.

## Does the boa have fangs?

No. Fangs are enlarged hollow teeth used for injecting poison. The boa has many long, solid teeth. It uses them to catch birds, bats, monkeys, pigs, and other animals.

## Heat sensors

Boas have pits in their lip scales that can sense, or detect, heat. These heat detectors can locate prey and guide the boa to it even in total darkness.

# How does a rattlesnake rattle?

The rattlesnake is known for its deadly poison and the rattle at the end of its tail. When it is alarmed, the snake shakes the rattle by waving its tail back and forth, thus warning intruders away.

## What is the rattle made of?

The rattlesnake's rattle is made of horny sections that look like small upside-down cups stacked loosely one on top of the other. When the snake's tail moves, these sections rub against each other and make a whirring, buzzing sound.

## Tell Me More

Each time the rattlesnake sheds its skin, a new section is added to its rattle.

Unlike many snakes, rattlesnakes give birth to live babies.

12

# Are sea serpents real?

Many years ago, sailors and fishermen told stories of huge sea serpents that capsized their boats and caused stormy seas. We now know that these were all imaginary tales told by frightened people.

Yet, strange as it may seem, there really are snakes living in the sea.

Sea snakes can dive deeper than a hundred feet and stay underwater for hours without coming up to breathe. Most give birth to live babies in the ocean and never leave the water.

## Tell Me More

Sea snakes have flat tails shaped like paddles, which help them move through the water.

## How do sea snakes breathe?

Since snakes have lungs, not gills, they must breathe air. Their nostrils are placed on top of their head, so they can come to the surface of the water to breathe without being seen by birds or other animals.

# Why does a lizard break off its tail?

Most lizards have four short legs, a short body, and a very long tail. When a predator tries to capture a lizard, it usually grasps the tail. But then the predator is in for a surprise. Though it has caught hold of the the lizard's tail, it may not have caught the lizard. That's because many kinds of lizards can break off their tail and escape. A new tail grows back before long.

## What's a glass snake?

A glass snake is a lizard with no legs. If an animal catches it by the tail, the tail may break into several pieces. Each piece wiggles and distracts the attacker while the lizard slithers off to safety.

## Tell Me More

Baby lizards cut their way out of their tough eggshells with a special *egg tooth* that grows on the top of their snout. The egg tooth falls off soon after the babies have hatched.

## More lizard magic tricks

- Geckos' tongues are so long that they can use them to wash their eyes.

- The blue-tongued skink lizard scares its enemies by sticking out its bright blue tongue.

- The spiny-tailed lizard's tail is covered with sharp spikes that discourage predators from grabbing it.

- Some lizards can change the color of their skin to blend with their surroundings. This is called *camouflage*.

**Amazing**
*but* TRUE

Gecko lizards sometimes grow two or three tails to replace the one that has been lost.

# Can reptiles fly?

Though reptiles can't actually fly, some can glide through the air to hunt for food or to escape their enemies. The flying gecko, the flying dragon, and the flying snake can all sail through the air. But none of them have real wings.

## The flying gecko

The flying gecko makes its home high in the branches of trees. Flying comes in handy far above the ground, and the gecko has the right equipment for air travel.

## Flaps up!

Geckos have flaps of skin that they can spread out like wings. When the gecko is ready to fly, it leaps into the air, spreads its flaps, and uses its flat tail to steer.

## What's a flying dragon?

The flying dragon, shown above, is quite a pilot. This lizard has flaps of skin on its sides that it can stretch out like wings. It can change the direction of its path in midair by changing the shape of the muscles in its skin flaps.

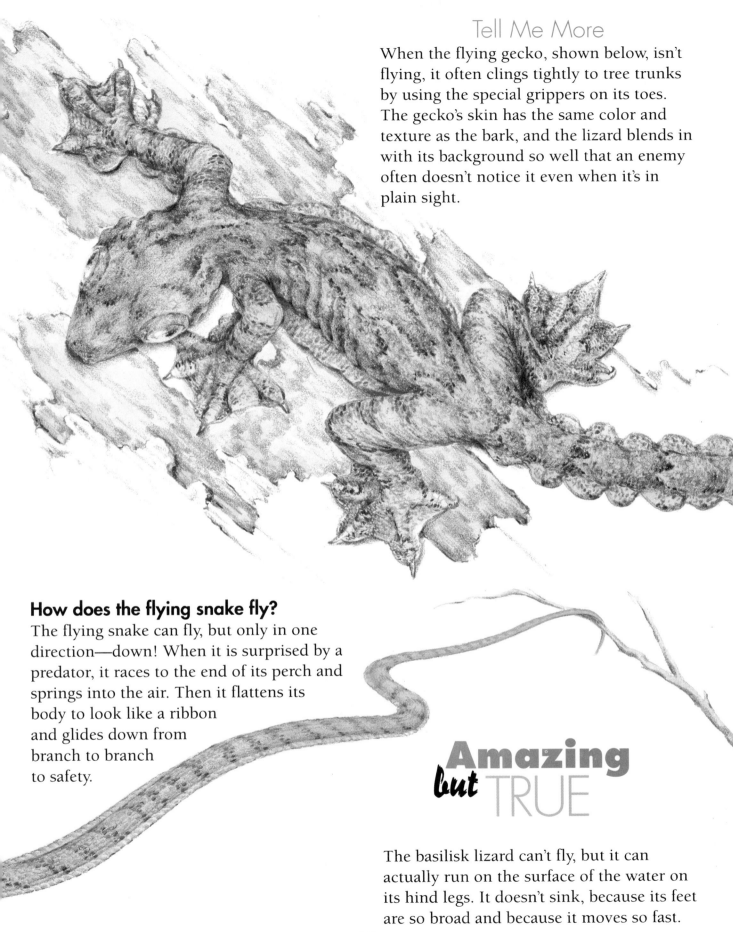

When the flying gecko, shown below, isn't flying, it often clings tightly to tree trunks by using the special grippers on its toes. The gecko's skin has the same color and texture as the bark, and the lizard blends in with its background so well that an enemy often doesn't notice it even when it's in plain sight.

## How does the flying snake fly?

The flying snake can fly, but only in one direction—down! When it is surprised by a predator, it races to the end of its perch and springs into the air. Then it flattens its body to look like a ribbon and glides down from branch to branch to safety.

## Amazing but TRUE

The basilisk lizard can't fly, but it can actually run on the surface of the water on its hind legs. It doesn't sink, because its feet are so broad and because it moves so fast.

17

# Is the iguana as fierce as it looks?

Iguanas are the biggest lizards living in the Americas—about four feet long, sometimes even more than six feet! They have a large green head and a comb of spines going down their back from head to tail. Though iguanas look ferocious, they are quite harmless and can become friendly. Some people in South America keep iguanas as pets.

## What do iguanas eat?

Young iguanas eat insects, but most adults are vegetarians, feeding only on plants and fruits. Desert iguanas have tough jaws and feed on cactus—spines and all. Many iguanas live in the tropical rainforest, climbing up and down trees with great speed. Marine iguanas hunt for food in the sea. They feed underwater, mostly on different kinds of seaweed.

## Fight or flight?

Though the iguana can use its powerful tail to defend itself, it usually shies away from fights. Since it is a good swimmer, it often chooses the river as a means of escape.

Some male iguanas have brightly colored skin flaps on the sides of their head. They spread these flaps to shock their enemies, or to attract females.

Amazing but TRUE

The rhinoceros iguana has horns on its snout. The older the animal is, the longer its horns are.

# Are dragons real?

Fire-breathing, flying dragons are creatures of the imagination. However, there are some amazing lizards, like the Komodo dragon and the water dragon, that look just like the dragons described in fairy tales and myths.

The Komodo dragon is the largest of all the lizards. Most lizards are less than a foot long, but the Komodo often reaches ten feet in length. It doesn't breathe fire and it doesn't have wings, but it certainly looks like a monster. The Komodo has a large head, a long tongue, a wrinkled neck, strong claws, and a long, thick tail. Like fairy–tale dragons, Komodos can hurt people, but they much prefer to go after wild pigs or deer.

The water dragon, which is shown on the cover, hunts for plants and insects in the jungles of New Guinea and Asia. Like the basilisk lizard, this remarkable creature has special feet that actually allow it to run on top of the water. The male water dragon—an agamid lizard—can be recognized by the beautiful crest at the the base of its tail.

Though it is not as large as the Komodo, the water dragon is every bit as spectacular as its giant relative.

# Why can't turtles jump?

Turtles are unusual because the top part of their body is fused with their shell. Their legs stick out through holes between the upper and lower shells, so they can't hop or jump. The turtle's thick, heavy shell may limit its ability to move, but it is good protection for its soft body.

## How does a turtle protect itself?

When turtles are frightened or attacked, there's really no need for them to jump away or even move very fast. Most just pull their head and feet into their shell and wait for their enemy to go away. Then they continue walking at their usual slow pace.

The snapping turtle can't draw its head and feet into its shell. But it can protect itself with its strong, sharp beak, which it uses to snap at predators and also to capture food.

The snake-necked turtle can't fit all of its long neck into its shell. When frightened, this turtle tucks its head and neck under the edge of its shell behind its front legs.

Tell Me More

The largest of all turtles live in the sea. Some sea turtles grow to a length of eight feet and weigh two thousand pounds. They spend most of their life in the water. Once every two or three years, the female hauls herself out of the water to lay her eggs in the sand.

## What is a turtle's shell made of?

A turtle's shell is made of two parts that are joined at each side of the turtle. The curved *carapace* covers its back, and the flat *plastron* protects its underside. Turtle shells come in many different shapes, colors, and patterns. Some look like boxes or domes, and others are flat. Some are as long as a yardstick, while others could fit in the palm of your hand.

Turtles eat both plants and meat. Yet they have no teeth! Their beaked jaws have sharp edges, which they use like knives for cutting food into pieces.

21

# Why does a chameleon change color?

Most chameleons are naturally green or brown, but they can change their color. The color these lizards become depends on how they feel, on the temperature, and on the amount of light.

Tell Me More

A chameleon can be hard to see because its color often blends in with its background.

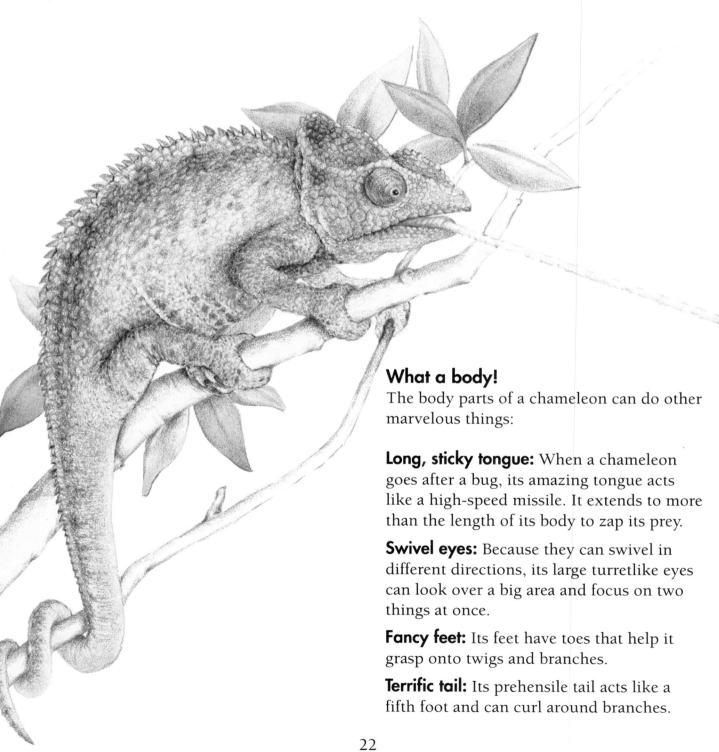

## What a body!

The body parts of a chameleon can do other marvelous things:

**Long, sticky tongue:** When a chameleon goes after a bug, its amazing tongue acts like a high-speed missile. It extends to more than the length of its body to zap its prey.

**Swivel eyes:** Because they can swivel in different directions, its large turretlike eyes can look over a big area and focus on two things at once.

**Fancy feet:** Its feet have toes that help it grasp onto twigs and branches.

**Terrific tail:** Its prehensile tail acts like a fifth foot and can curl around branches.

22

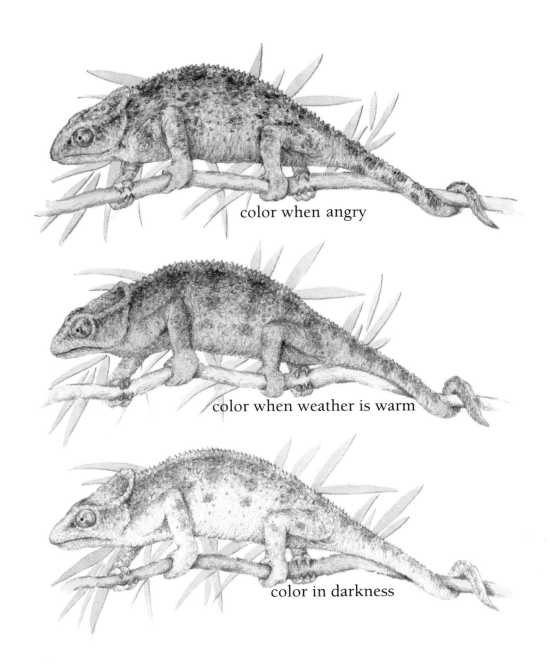

color when angry

color when weather is warm

color in darkness

## What do the colors mean?

You can tell how chameleons feel by their color. When chameleons get angry, they usually turn a darker shade. When they are depressed or sick, they may turn black. And when all is well, they may often be a calm green color. You can tell how hot or cold, light or dark, it is by the way chameleons look. When it is warm, they are dark green. When it is dark, they are pale. When the weather is cool, they are usually light green.

**Amazing** *but* TRUE

If part of a chameleon is in the shade and part in the sun, it will have two different colors. If a leaf shades part of a chameleon's body, that part will have a leaf shape imprinted on it.

23

# What are crocodile tears?

According to legend, crocodiles shed tears after they have swallowed a person to show they are sorry. But crocodiles don't cry. They are among the most ferocious of all living reptiles. They hunt and devour all kinds of animals, including human beings.

## What's the difference between a crocodile and an alligator?

Crocodiles and alligators belong to a group of animals called *crocodilians*. There are several ways to tell them apart. The easiest way is to look at them when their mouth is closed. If you can see one large tooth sticking out on each side of the snout, you're looking at a crocodile.

## What big teeth you have!

Crocodiles and alligators use their sharp teeth to capture their prey, but they never use them for chewing.

When a crocodile fights its prey, it often loses many of its teeth. But that doesn't seem to bother it at all, because crocodiles and alligators grow many more new sets of teeth in their lifetime.

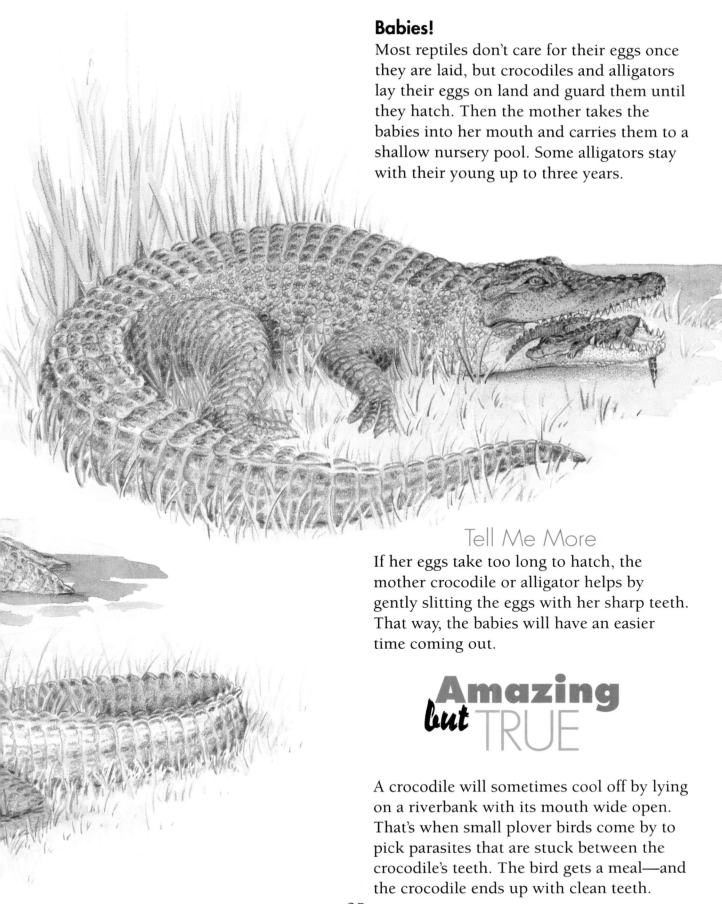

## Babies!

Most reptiles don't care for their eggs once they are laid, but crocodiles and alligators lay their eggs on land and guard them until they hatch. Then the mother takes the babies into her mouth and carries them to a shallow nursery pool. Some alligators stay with their young up to three years.

### Tell Me More

If her eggs take too long to hatch, the mother crocodile or alligator helps by gently slitting the eggs with her sharp teeth. That way, the babies will have an easier time coming out.

### Amazing but TRUE

A crocodile will sometimes cool off by lying on a riverbank with its mouth wide open. That's when small plover birds come by to pick parasites that are stuck between the crocodile's teeth. The bird gets a meal—and the crocodile ends up with clean teeth.

# What is a newt?

salamander

Newts and salamanders are amphibians with tails. They resemble lizards, but their skin is moist and soft, rather than dry and scaly. Their front feet each have four toes and one claw, while a lizard has five toes—all with claws.

Most newts and salamanders start life in a fishlike form, swimming in ponds and streams. At this stage of their development, they breathe with gills instead of lungs. As they grow, most lose their gills, develop lungs, and change into creatures that can live on land.

newt

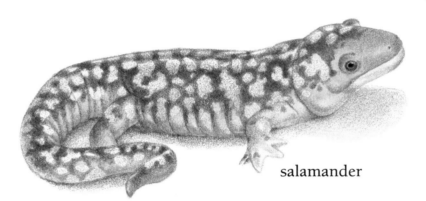

salamander

newt

## Amazing but TRUE

The red–bellied newt has a bright–orange belly. When it is angry or alarmed, it flips its tail over its back to show its bright underside. That often scares predators away.

newt

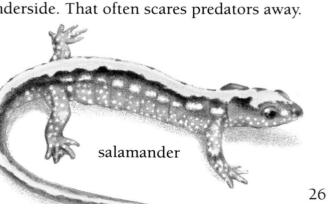

salamander

newt

26

# Why do  leap?

Frogs and toads have something that no other amphibian or reptile has: two long, powerful hind legs specially designed for leaping away from danger. But these hind legs are not only for leaping. They are also powerful aids when it comes to swimming. In fact, human swimmers often wear froglike flippers and imitate the frog's kick to propel themselves forward.

## Amazing but TRUE

The poison dart frog of South America produces a deadly poison in its skin. Some Indians in the Amazon dip their blowgun darts into the frog's poison when they go hunting. Animals shot with these darts collapse in just a few minutes.

## Tell Me More

Like salamanders and newts, frogs and toads are amphibians. But salamanders and newts have long tails, while frogs and toads lose their tails when they change from tadpoles to land dwellers.

# How does a tadpole become a frog?

You may know the story of the Frog Prince, in which a common frog magically turns into a man. Of course that is a fairy tale. But the true-life story of a frog is just as surprising. Frogs—and toads—start life in the water, looking and behaving like fish. As they grow, they slowly change into their adult form, equipped to live on land. This process of change is called *metamorphosis*.

A frog's metamorphosis begins with an egg, which the female lays in the water in early spring. From late spring through early summer, the baby frog hatches and remains in the water as its body grows and changes form. The metamorphosis is usually complete by midsummer, when the little froglet is ready to hop on land. Here's what happens:

2 After several days to a week, little wiggly creatures, called tadpoles, hatch from the eggs. The tadpoles are baby frogs, but they don't look like their parents. They have fishlike bodies and no legs. They live in water and breathe through gills, not lungs.

1 The mother frog lays her eggs in the water. They look like tiny spots inside a clear jellylike mass. The jelly helps keep the eggs from sinking. It also acts like a magnifying lens, concentrating the rays of the sun to keep the eggs warm.

4 Then their tail gets shorter and front legs appear. They are beginning to look a little like frogs.

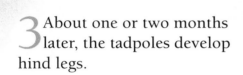

3 About one or two months later, the tadpoles develop hind legs.

5 Next, the tadpoles develop lungs and lose their gills.

6 Finally, they become adults.

## Amazing but TRUE

Some jungle frogs live high up in the treetops. They don't lay their eggs on the water, where fish and insects could eat them. Instead, they lay their eggs on leaves that hang above the water. When the tadpoles hatch, they slide off the leaves and drop into the water below. Then they swim away.

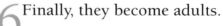

# What on earth is a tuatara?

There are many, many different kinds of snakes, turtles, lizards, and crocodiles, but the tuatara is in a group all by itself. The tuatara is the only remaining example of a reptile that lived one hundred forty million years ago in the time of dinosaurs—long, long before monkeys, horses, elephants, or human beings existed.

Like its ancestors, the tuatara has a huge head, a crest of horny spines running all the way down its back, short strong legs, and five claws on each of its feet. Its snout forms a kind of beak, and its eyes have pupils that look like vertical lines.

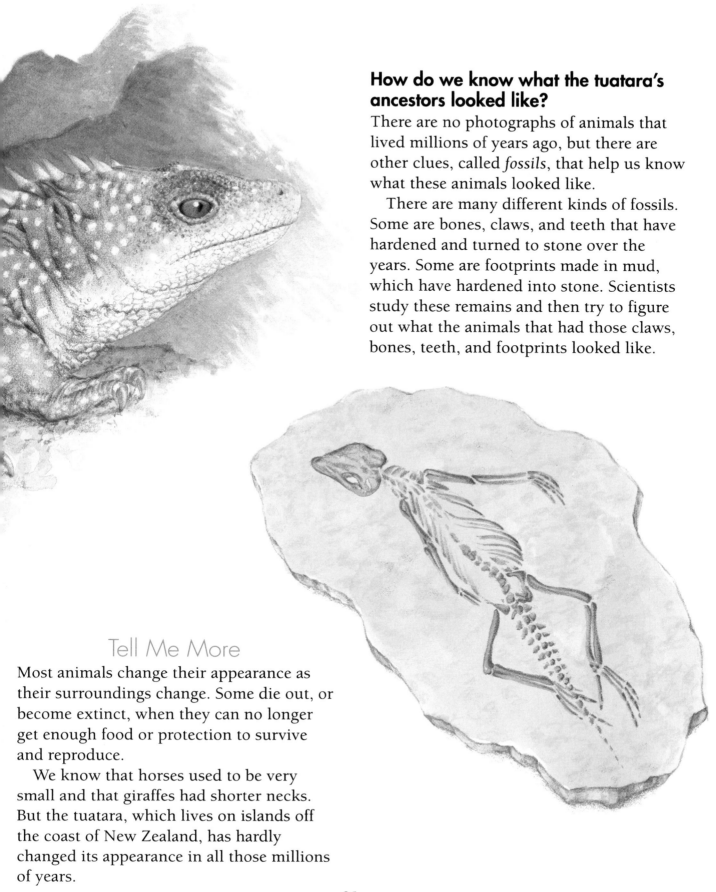

## How do we know what the tuatara's ancestors looked like?

There are no photographs of animals that lived millions of years ago, but there are other clues, called *fossils*, that help us know what these animals looked like.

There are many different kinds of fossils. Some are bones, claws, and teeth that have hardened and turned to stone over the years. Some are footprints made in mud, which have hardened into stone. Scientists study these remains and then try to figure out what the animals that had those claws, bones, teeth, and footprints looked like.

## Tell Me More

Most animals change their appearance as their surroundings change. Some die out, or become extinct, when they can no longer get enough food or protection to survive and reproduce.

We know that horses used to be very small and that giraffes had shorter necks. But the tuatara, which lives on islands off the coast of New Zealand, has hardly changed its appearance in all those millions of years.

# Tell Me More

Though you have come to the last page of this book, you are only beginning to know about the wonderful true-life stories of reptiles and amphibians. Scientists who study reptiles are called *herpetologists*. But you don't have to be a herpetologist to enjoy finding out more about these amazing members of the animal kingdom.

There seems to be a plan and a purpose for everything in nature. Large or small, beautiful or strange, each plant and animal has a role to fulfill. Each has an effect on something else that sooner or later has an effect on us.

Here are some more amazing-but-true facts that should start you on your way to new discoveries:

- The Gila monster is an unusual lizard that lives in the North American desert. When food is plentiful, this lizard eats so much that it forms a big lump of fat that is stored in its tail. When food is scarce, the Gila monster lives off the stored fat. Despite its ability to adapt to the most difficult natural conditions, the Gila monster won't survive if people continue to invade its desert habitat.

- Male box turtles have red eyes; females have yellow eyes.

- Some jungle frogs live high up in the treetops. They lay their eggs on leaves that hang above a marsh or river. When the tadpoles hatch, they slide off the leaves, drop into the water below, and swim away.

- The alligator snapping turtle has a growth on its tongue that looks like a pink worm. When a fish comes to eat the "worm," the turtle snaps its mouth shut and eats the fish.

# INDEX